The Biggest Christmas Tree

by David Gantz

SCHOLASTIC INC.
New York Toronto London Auckland Sydney

It was Christmas vacation.
Everyone was very excited.

2

"Yes," said Zelda. "We can set it up here and decorate it."

3

"I know where we can find a tree," said Denny. "Follow me."

START

4

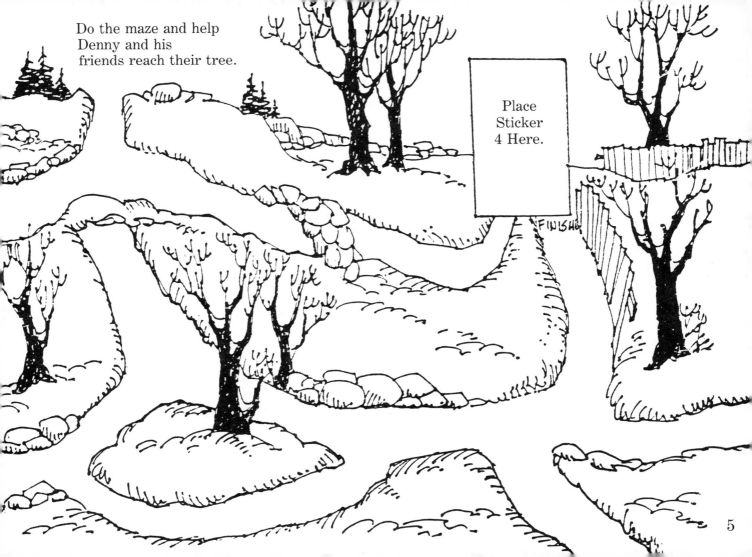

Do the maze and help Denny and his friends reach their tree.

Place Sticker 4 Here.

FINISH

When they brought the tree back, they were all disappointed.

"I know where we can get a really *big* Christmas tree," said Zelda.

"Pine Tree Ridge!" shouted Suzie.

"But that means we have to pass Old Man Johnson's Junkyard!" added Jackie.

"And you know what's there!" cried Denny.

Zelda wondered what danger there was in the junkyard.

Connect the dots to see what Zelda thought it was.

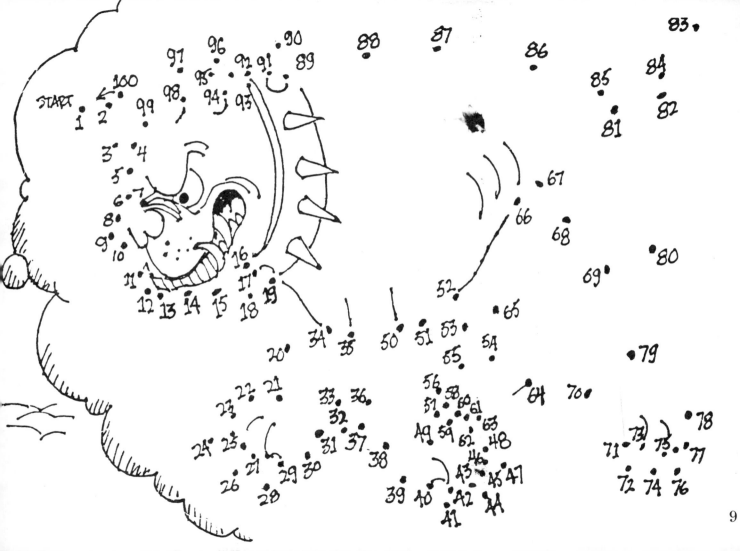

9

"There are four vicious guard dogs at the junkyard," said Denny.

They all tried to imagine how the dogs looked. . . .

Place Sticker 9 Here.

Place Sticker 10 Here.

Place Sticker 11 Here.

Place Sticker 12 Here.

Place Sticker 13 Here.

Place Sticker 14 Here.

Place Sticker 15 Here.

Place Sticker 16 Here.

11

In order to forget how scared they were, they told dog jokes.

I heard you took your dog to the Flea Circus.

Place Sticker 17 Here.

Did you hear about the kid that bit the dog?

Hold these pages up to a mirror to see the answers.

12

13

14

Hey, I know how we can

Place Sticker 21 Here.

the Junkyard.

Circle every other letter to find out
what Suzie is saying.
The first letter is circled for you.

15

Help Suzie and the kids get to
Pine Tree Ridge without passing
the junkyard.

There are 92 gummed stickers in this book. Some are numbered, some are not. Follow the instructions inside to find out where the numbered stickers belong. All the stickers are perforated. Carefully tear them out, moisten, and place numbered stickers as shown. Then read and color the pages. When you are finished, you will find lots of stickers remaining. Use these extra stickers to decorate your own Christmas cards.

18 Yes, he was eating a frankfurter.

1 [owl] –OL+ [eye] –Y+K

2 CH+ [hand] –W+ MAS

19 Only as long as he keeps barking.

5 [tie] + [wrist]

6 [ruler] –T [candy cane] [garland]

3 [tree]

HAPPY HOLIDAYS

17 Yes and he stole the show!

MERRY CHRISTMAS

MERRY CHRISTMAS

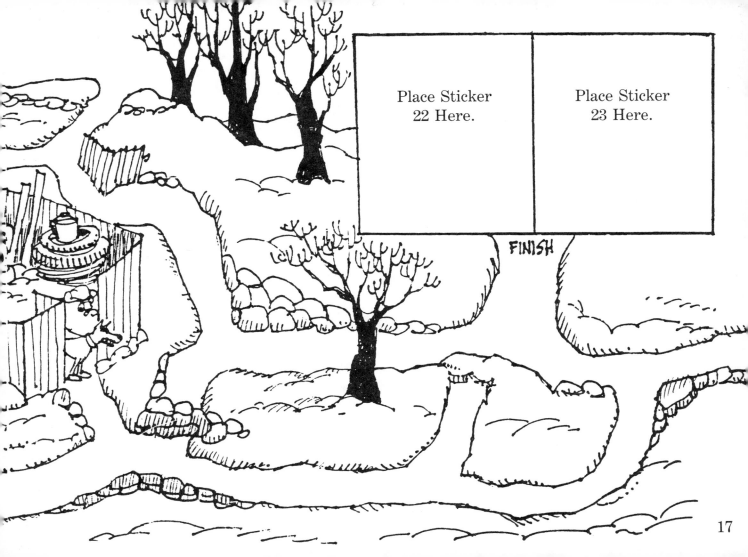

Place Sticker
22 Here.

Place Sticker
23 Here.

FINISH

17

When they got to Pine Tree Ridge,
Denny said, "Wow, that's great!"

Jackie said, "It's huge!"

And Zelda was so surprised that her
words came out scrambled.

O	W	N		T	A	T	H		S	I		A
2	3	1		4	3	1	2		2	1		1

___ ___ ___   ___ ___ ___ ___   ___ ___   ___

S	R	I	T	H	S	C	A	M		E	R	E	T
5	3	4	6	2	9	1	8	7		4	2	3	1

___ ___ ___ ___ ___ ___ ___ ___ ___   ___ ___ ___ ___

Use the numbers to unscramble the words.

They all imagined how they
would decorate such a
beautiful tree.

20

Decorate the tree with some of the
stickers that are *not* numbered.

21

"Now, how do we chop it down and get it to our tree house?" asked Jackie.

"It's too pretty to chop down," replied Suzie.

"Hey, I know how to get the tree to our tree house without having to chop it down!" cried Zelda.

To see what Zelda has in mind, connect the dots.

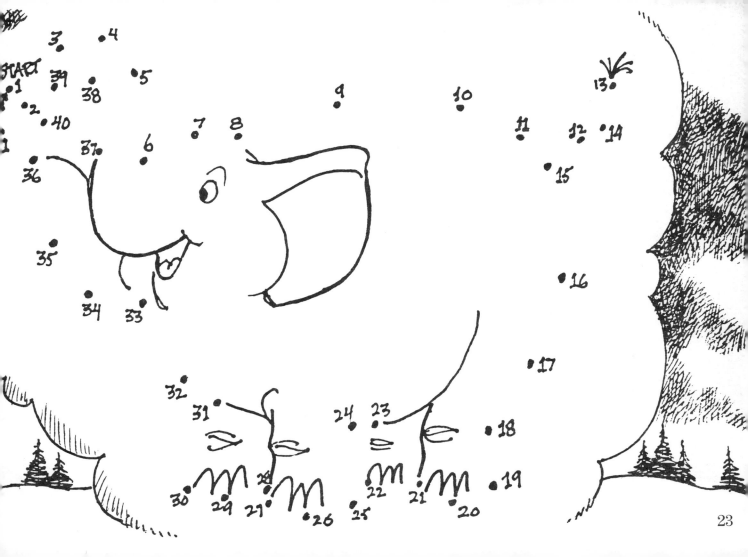

23

Color this scene.

When they told Elsie's trainer what they wanted to do, he said:

"Elsie would be happy to help her Valentine's Day friends."

Place Sticker
25 Here.

Place Sticker
26 Here.

Place Sticker
27 Here.

Place Sticker
28 Here.

27

Elsie pulled up the tree,
roots and all, and carried it to
the tree house where Denny
and Jackie dug a deep hole.

After the tree was planted, Elsie helped them reach the upper branches to hang the decorations.

Add some decoration stickers that are *not* numbered.

On Christmas Eve, all of the Tree House Kids and Elsie gathered around their beautiful Christmas tree to sing carols.

Add some decoration stickers that are *not* numbered.

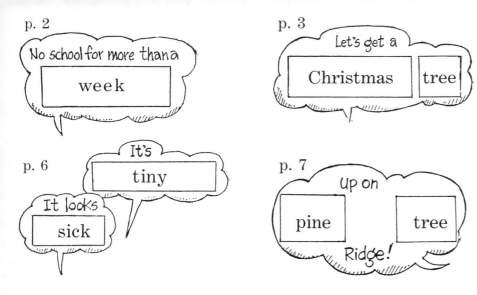

p. 2 — No school for more than a **week**

p. 3 — Let's get a **Christmas** **tree**

p. 6 — It looks **sick** It's **tiny**

p. 7 — **pine** Up on **tree** Ridge!

Here are the answers.

ISBN 0-590-44026-8

Copyright © 1990 by David Gantz.
All rights reserved. Published by Scholastic Inc.

12 11 10 9 8 7 6 5 4 3 2 1   0 1 2 3 4 5/9

Printed in the U.S.A.
First Scholastic printing, November 1990   41